WORLD FAMOUS MURIEL and THE MAGIC MYSTERY

by Sue Alexander
illustrated by Marla Frazee

Thomas Y. Crowell   New York

For Sid Fleischman—
Writer, Magician and Friend Extraordinaire

S.A.

To Tim

M.F.

World Famous Muriel and the Magic Mystery
Text copyright © 1990 by Sue Alexander
Illustrations copyright © 1990 by Marla Frazee
Printed in the U.S.A. All rights reserved.
10 9 8 7 6 5 4 3 2 1
First Edition

Library of Congress Cataloging-in-Publication Data
Alexander, Sue, 1933–
    World famous Muriel and the magic mystery / by Sue Alexander ;
illustrated by Marla Frazee.
        p.   cm.
    Summary: World Famous Muriel earns her reputation again when,
with the help of numerous peanut butter cookies, she finds the
Great Hokus Pokus after he disappears in the middle of rehearsing
for his magic show.
    ISBN 0-690-04787-8 : $. — ISBN 0-690-04789-4 (lib. bdg.) :
$
    [1. Magicians—Fiction.   2. Mystery and detective stories.]
I. Frazee, Marla, ill.   II. Title.
PZ7.A3784Wp 1990   89-22396
[E]—dc20   CIP
                                                          AC

Early one morning Muriel found a note on her
doorstep. It said:

Dear World Famous Muriel,
The Great Hokus Pokus will put on his Magic Show at
my theater today. He is going to practice some new
magic tricks this morning. Please come and watch.
                                    Your friend,
                        Professor M. C. Ballyhoo

"That sounds like fun," Muriel said. "I will go."

And off she went.

The Great Hokus Pokus stood in the middle of the
stage.
He bowed.

Then he waved his magic wand.
"ABRA! CADABRA! KAZOOM!" he said.
And rabbits came out of his hat.
Muriel clapped.
The Great Hokus Pokus waved his magic wand again.
"ZIM! ZAM! ZERKO!" he said.

And the rabbits turned into balloons.
Muriel cheered.

The Great Hokus Pokus waved his magic wand once
more.

"DIZZLE! DAZZLE! KABOOM!" he said.

Nothing happened.

The balloons did not change into anything.

"DIZZLE! DAZZLE! KABOOM!" said the Great
Hokus Pokus again.

The balloons still stayed balloons.

"Hmmm," said the Great Hokus Pokus.

He scratched his head.

Then he waved his magic wand again.

"WHIM! WHAM! WHOOSH!" said the Great
Hokus Pokus.

The balloons disappeared.

So did the Great Hokus Pokus.
After a while Muriel said, "Somehow, I do not think
this is part of the show."

Professor Ballyhoo ran onto the stage.

He looked behind all the curtains.

"Where are you, Great Hokus Pokus?" he called.

There was no answer.

"Oh, dear," said the Professor. "What am I going to do? Everyone will be here soon to see the Great Hokus Pokus. And I can't find him!"

Then he looked at Muriel.

"Muriel," he said, "you are the best tightrope walker in the world. You are World Famous. You are also very smart. You are World Famous for that, too. Can you find the Great Hokus Pokus?"

"Of course," Muriel said. "I will think very hard. I will think of why the Great Hokus Pokus disappeared. Then I will know where to find him."

"Hooray!" said the Professor.

"There is just one thing," Muriel said. "I do my best thinking while I am eating peanut-butter cookies."

"I'll get you some," said the Professor.

And he did.

Muriel ate a cookie.

Then she went to the middle of the stage.
The Professor stood next to her.
"Hmmm," Muriel said.
She tapped her foot.

"Help!" yelled the Professor. "I'm sliding!"

Muriel landed on the floor.

The Professor landed on Muriel.

"Muriel," he said, "I'm afraid to look. Did we slide into another world?"

"No," Muriel said. "We slid into the basement."

"That's a relief!" said the Professor.

And he opened his eyes.

"I have thought of how the Great Hokus Pokus disappeared," Muriel said.

"How?" asked the Professor.

"The same way we did," Muriel said.

"Oh," said the Professor.

Muriel ate another cookie.

Then she started to look around the basement.
So did the Professor.

Suddenly he stopped.

"Help!" he yelled. "A ghost! It's floating in the air!"
And he ran behind a post.

"Don't be scared, Professor," Muriel said. "It's not a real ghost."
"It's not?" said the Professor. "Then what is it?"
"A sheet," Muriel said.
And she pulled it out of the air.

The Professor came out from behind the post.
"I have thought of who made the sheet float in the air," Muriel said.
"Who?" asked the Professor.
"The Great Hokus Pokus, that's who," answered Muriel. "Making things float in the air is a magic trick."
"Oh my, so it is," said the Professor.
He looked around.
"Great Hokus Pokus," he called, "are you here?"
There was no answer.

Muriel ate a cookie.

Then she said, "I have thought of something. Where there is one magic trick, there are probably others."

"Not more floating, ghosts, I hope," said the Professor. "One of those is enough."

And he shivered.

"If we look through his magic tricks," Muriel went on, "we may find out *why* the Great Hokus Pokus disappeared. And then we will know where to find him."

"That is good thinking! You *are* smart, Muriel," said the Professor.

"I know," Muriel said.

And she ate another cookie.

Then she looked for some more magic tricks.

She found lots of them.

"I remember these tricks," said the Professor. "The Great Hokus Pokus tried, but he could not make some of them work."

"Hmmm," Muriel said.

She looked at the magic tricks.

She ate some more cookies.

Then she said. "I know where to find the Great
Hokus Pokus."
And out of the basement she went.
"Wait for me!" called the Professor.
And he ran after Muriel.

Muriel went up one block and down another.
She turned the corner.
Then she stopped.

"Muriel, this is the library!" said the Professor.
"Yes," Muriel said. "And the Great Hokus Pokus is inside."
The Professor hurried into the library.

He saw a sign on the desk.

"Magicians like rabbits," said the Professor. "That's
where I will find the Great Hokus Pokus!"
And he ran to the courtyard.

But he did not see the Great Hokus Pokus.
"Oh dear!" said the Professor.
Then he saw another sign.
It said:

      Stories About Magic in the Story Circle.

"Magicians would like stories about magic," said the
Professor. "*That* must be where I will find the Great
Hokus Pokus."

And he hurried to the story circle.

But he did not see the Great Hokus Pokus there, either.

"Where can he be?" wailed the Professor. "I will never find the Great Hokus Pokus in time for the Magic Show. I will have to call it off!"
And he began to cry.

"Don't cry, Professor," Muriel said. "Follow me."

Muriel went past the shelves
full of magazines.

She went past the dictionaries.

She went past the shelves
marked "Plays."
Then she stopped.
The Professor looked over
Muriel's shoulder.

And he saw the Great Hokus Pokus.

"Hooray!" yelled the Professor.

Then he said, "Muriel, how did you know that the Great Hokus Pokus was here?"

"I thought very hard," Muriel said. "I thought that the Great Hokus Pokus did not know how to do some of his magic tricks."

"That's true," said the Professor.

"So I thought," Muriel said, "that he would want to find out how to do them. You can find out lots of things in books. Even how to do magic tricks."

"So you can," agreed the Professor.

"The library has lots of books," Muriel went on.

"And that's why I thought we would find the Great Hokus Pokus here."

"Oh Muriel, you are so smart!" said the Professor.

"I know," Muriel said.

And she ate some more cookies.

A little while later, the Great Hokus Pokus stood in
the middle of the stage.

He bowed.
He waved his magic wand.
"ABRA! CADABRA!
KAZOOM!" he said.
And rabbits came out of his hat.
Everyone clapped.

The Great Hokus Pokus waved
his magic wand again.
"ZIM! ZAM! ZERKO!"
he said.
And the rabbits turned into
balloons.
Everyone cheered.

The Great Hokus Pokus waved
his magic wand once more.
"DIZZLE! DAZZLE!
KABOOM!" he said.
And the balloons turned into
peanut butter cookies.
Everyone whistled.
"WHIM! WHAM!
WHOOSH!" said the Great
Hokus Pokus.

And World Famous Muriel made the cookies
disappear.

D